Lord of the universe: I am a simple man, an ignorant man. Oh, how I wish I had the words to fashion beautiful prayers to praise thee! But alas, I cannot find the words. So, listen to me, O God, as I recite the alphabet. You know what I think and how I feel. Take these letters of the alphabet and you form the words to express the yearning, the love for thee, that is in my heart.

UNKNOWN

Giving Thanks

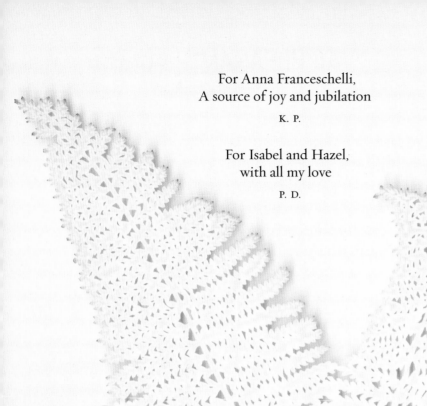

For Anna Franceschelli,
A source of joy and jubilation

K. P.

For Isabel and Hazel,
with all my love

P. D.

Original text © 2013 by Minna Murra, Inc.
Illustrations © 2013 by Pamela Dalton.

Acknowledgments of permission to reprint previously published materials appear on page 53, which constitutes as an extension of this copyright page.

Library of Congress Cataloging-in-Publication Data available.

ISBN 978-1-4521-1339-5

Manufactured in China.

FSC
MIX
Paper from responsible sources
www.fsc.org   FSC® C104723

Design by Amelia May Mack.
Calligraphy by Anne Robin.
Photographs by Matthew Carden.
Typeset in Hoefler & Frere-Jones Requiem.

10 9 8 7 6 5 4 3 2 1

Handprint Books
is an imprint of
Chronicle Books LLC
680 Second Street
San Francisco, CA 94107
www.chroniclekids.com

Giving Thanks

POEMS, PRAYERS, AND
PRAISE SONGS OF THANKSGIVING

Edited and with reflections by
KATHERINE PATERSON

Illustrations by
PAMELA DALTON

HANDPRINT BOOKS

an imprint of Chronicle Books
San Francisco

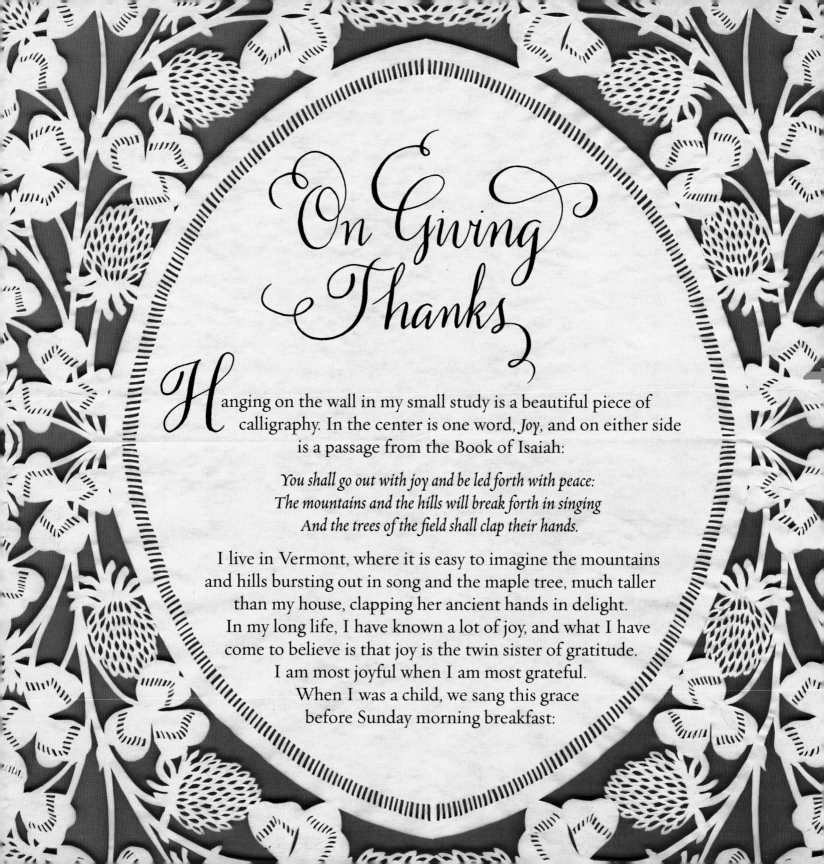

On Giving Thanks

Hanging on the wall in my small study is a beautiful piece of calligraphy. In the center is one word, *Joy*, and on either side is a passage from the Book of Isaiah:

You shall go out with joy and be led forth with peace:
The mountains and the hills will break forth in singing
And the trees of the field shall clap their hands.

I live in Vermont, where it is easy to imagine the mountains and hills bursting out in song and the maple tree, much taller than my house, clapping her ancient hands in delight. In my long life, I have known a lot of joy, and what I have come to believe is that joy is the twin sister of gratitude. I am most joyful when I am most grateful. When I was a child, we sang this grace before Sunday morning breakfast:

Thank you for the world so sweet,
Thank you for the food we eat,
Thank you for the birds that sing,
Thank you, God, for everything.

And I am thankful, three times every day, for good food to eat and a warm home. I am grateful for the beauty of each season, from the brightness of summer to the snows of winter. I am grateful for the many years I have been given to enjoy this good earth—for my loving family, my crazy dog, my church, my friends, and for work I love to do that has given me friends all around the world. I am truly blessed.

But my childhood blessing reminds me to be thankful for everything—not just those occasions when I am happy, but the hard times—the disappointments, failures, and losses that brought me to a new place where I could grow in wisdom and compassion and, yes, real joy. This is a book about giving thanks—thanks for everything. The prayers on these pages come from many ages and multiple traditions, but I think you will find, as I have, a kinship with these voices and inspiration from the pictures that accompany them. I know words and art will help me consider all the blessings I have been given, remembering the prayer of seventeenth-century poet George Herbert, and making it my own:

Thou that hast given so much to me, give one
thing more—a grateful heart.

KATHERINE PATERSON

Gather Around the Table

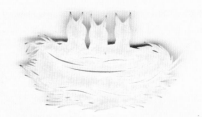

The other day I peeled an orange and divided it into sections. The aroma seemed to fill the kitchen. The first bite was just as delicious as the smell of it had promised. But then I got distracted, and the next thing I knew I was looking down at an empty plate. I had eaten the whole orange without realizing it, much less enjoying it or being grateful for it.

It made me remember the story of a Japanese friend. She and her family had suffered terribly during World War II. Her children were so hungry that one day she took out her wedding kimono and traded it for two tomatoes.

In my family we have plenty to eat, and we try always to be thankful for that abundance. It is our habit at every meal to hold hands around the table as my husband, John, leads the prayer, beginning with the words "O Lord, bless this food and the hands that prepared it." Since those hands are most often mine, I like that, but I know that it is not just my hands that brought this food to the table. There are the farmers, like my friends, the Paquins; the grocer, like my friend, Jim Taylor; and many more whose names and contributions I'll never know—not to mention the sun, the rain, the good earth, and the plants and animals whose lives nourish my life.

If I think of everything and everyone who helped bring a meal to my table, I am overwhelmed with gratitude. But that is good. Meister Eckhart, who died almost seven hundred years ago, said, "If the only prayer you ever say in your entire life is 'thank you,' it will be enough."

K. P.

TO BE SAID WHILE HOLDING HANDS:

May the love that is in my heart
pass from my hand to yours.

TRADITIONAL AMERICAN GRACE

O you who believe!
Eat of the good things that we have provided
for you, and be grateful to Allah, if
it is indeed He whom you worship.

ISLAMIC PRAYER

When eating bamboo shoots,
remember the man who planted them.

CHINESE PROVERB

Mother Earth, you who give us food,
whose children we are and on whom we depend,
please make this produce you give us flourish
and make our children and our animals grow. . . .
Our parents tell us, "Children, the earth is the mother of man,
because she gives him food."

RIGOBERTA MENCHÚ (B. 1959)

For each new morning with its light,
For rest and shelter of the night,
For health and food,
For love and friends,
For everything Thy goodness sends.

RALPH WALDO EMERSON (1803–1882),
"THANKSGIVING"

Earth who gives to us this food,
Sun who makes it ripe and good,
Dearest Earth and Dearest Sun.
We'll not forget what you have done.

CHRISTIAN MORGENSTERN (1871–1914),
"THE WALDORF VERSE"

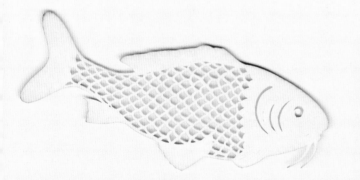

Now that I am about to eat, O Great Spirit,
Give my thanks to the beasts and birds
Whom you have provided for my hunger;
And pray deliver my sorrow
That living things must make a sacrifice
For my comfort and well-being.
Let the feather of corn spring up in its time
And let it not wither but make full grains
For the fires of our cooking pots,
Now that I am about to eat.

NATIVE AMERICAN GRACE

13

Some hae meat and canna eat,
And some wad eat that want it;
But we hae meat and we can eat,
And sae the Lord be thank it.

ROBERT BURNS (1759–1796),
"THE SELKIRK GRACE"

So I may raise corn,
So I may raise beans,
So I may raise wheat,
So I may raise squash,
So that with all good fortune
     I may be blessed.

PUEBLO BLESSING

Heaven,
Please make the rain fall,
So I have water to drink;
So I may plow my rice field;
So I may have my bowl of rice;
And my fish in great slices.

VIETNAMESE FARMERS' PRAYER

Blessed be the Creator
and all creative hands
which plant and harvest,
pack and haul and hand
over sustenance—
Blessed be carrot and cow,
potato and mushroom,
tomato and bean,
parsley and peas,
onion and thyme,
garlic and bay leaf,
pepper and water,
marjoram and oil,
and blessed be fire—
and blessed be the enjoyment
of nose and eye,
and blessed be color—
and blessed be the Creator
for the miracle of red potato,
for the miracle of green bean
for the miracle of fawn mushrooms,
and blessed be God
for the miracle of earth:
ancestors, grass, bird,
deer and all gone,
wild creatures
whose bodies become
carrots, peas, and wild
flowers, whose bodies give sustenance
to human hands, whose

agile dance of music
nourishes the ear
and soul of the dog
resting under the stove
and the woman working over
the stove and the geese
out the open window
strolling in the backyard.
And blessed be God for
all, all, all.

ALLA RENÉE BOZARTH (B. 1947),
"BLESSING OF THE STEW POT"

15

A buzzy bee came to eat—
what was I to do?
I let him have a bite or two—
then he was content too.
Thank You, God, for food to eat and to share.

Dear Lord,
Help me to live right now
in this moment of time
You have given me.

MARIAN WRIGHT EDELMAN (B. 1939),
TWO PRAYERS FROM "GRATITUDE"

Our Father which art in heaven, Hallowed be Thy name.
Thy kingdom come, Thy will be done in earth, as it is in heaven.
Give us this day our daily bread.
And forgive us our debts, as we forgive our debtors.
And lead us not into temptation, but deliver us from evil: For thine
is the kingdom, and the power, and the glory, for ever. Amen.

"THE LORD'S PRAYER," MATTHEW 6:9–13, KING JAMES VERSION

'Tis the gift to be simple, 'tis the gift to be free,
'Tis the gift to come down where we ought to be,
And when we find ourselves in the place just right,
'Twill be in the valley of love and delight.

When true simplicity is gain'd,
To bow and to bend we shan't be asham'd,
To turn, turn will be our delight,
Till by turning, turning we come round right.

SHAKER SONG BY ELDER JOSEPH BRACKETT (1797–1882),
"SIMPLE GIFTS"

Be a gardener,
dig and ditch,
toil and sweat,
and turn the earth upside down
and seek the deepness
and water the plants in time.
Continue this labor
and make sweet floods to run
and noble and abundant fruits
to spring.
Take this food and drink
and carry it to God
as your true worship.

JULIAN OF NORWICH (CA. 1342–1416)

Bless, O God, my little cow,
Bless, O God, my desire;
Bless Thou my partnership
And the milking of my hands, O God.

Bless, O God, each teat,
Bless, O God, each finger;
Bless Thou each drop
That goes into my pitcher, O God!

GAELIC BLESSING

A
Celebration
of Life

*I*t was August and there wasn't a breath of air coming in through the open windows, only the raucous humming of millions of cicadas who had, spitefully it seemed, chosen this very day to make their storied once-in-seventeen-years ascent from the earth to fill the air with their infernal racket and cover the ground with their brown husks.

At noontime my son David burst into the house. "I got this cicada about to bust its skin. Come watch." His excitement forced me to obey. Now you would think that a cicada, after seventeen years under the dark ground and with barely two days to live in the sunlight, would burst out of its shell in no time, but we learned better.

There was the tiny split that David had spotted earlier, and then, as though it had pulled down a waist-length zipper, we saw a hint of color. The extremities turned brown as limbs were eased out of the old armor. The buggy eyes dulled as the living ones withdrew. We began to count the colors that miraculously emerged from the dead shell— a pure Caribbean green, yellow, aqua, cream, beige, and flecks of gold bejeweling the head.

When almost out, its wings bits of crumpled ribbon stuck to its sides, our cicada still clung to its brown sarcophagus, which seemed half again too small for its now-splendid body. By this time we had watched for nearly an hour, forgetting the heat and noise, our whole selves stilled, captivated by this metamorphosis. At long last it stretched its wings, and suddenly, in the only swift movement we had seen, our cicada swung itself from the discarded husk onto the twig from which it hung. We left it then, checking back from time to time. At about four, we found the twig deserted. Our cicada had flown away to sing and breed and die, oblivious to the wake of wonder it had left behind.

In the fourteenth century, St. Julian of Norwich had a similar experience gazing at a hazelnut in the palm of her hand.

"I looked upon it with the eye of my understanding, and thought, 'What may this be?' And it was answered generally thus, 'It is all that is made.' I marveled how it might last, for I thought it might suddenly have fallen to nothing for littleness. And I was answered in my understanding: It lasts and ever shall, for God loves it. And so have all things their beginning by the love of God."

K. P.

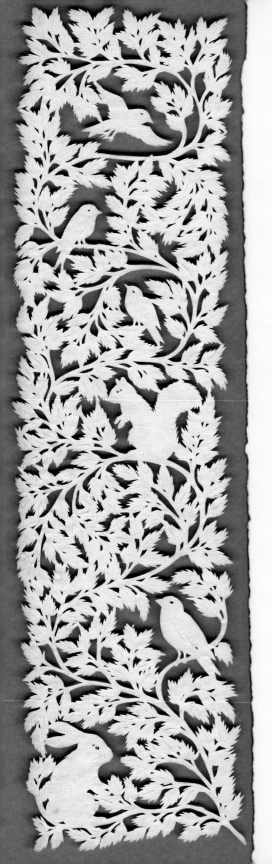

Morning has broken, like the first morning
Blackbird has spoken, like the first bird
Praise for the singing, praise for the morning
Praise for them springing fresh from the Word.

Sweet the rain's new fall, sunlit from heaven
Like the first dewfall, on the first grass
Praise for the sweetness of the wet garden
Sprung in completeness where His feet pass.

Mine is the sunlight, mine is the morning
Born of the one light, Eden saw play
Praise with elation, praise every morning
God's re-creation of the new day.

ELEANOR FARJEON (1881–1965),
FROM "MORNING HAS BROKEN"

As Thou hast set the moon in the sky to be
the poor man's lantern,
So let Thy light shine in my dark life
and lighten my path;
as the rice is sown in the water
and brings forth grain in great abundance,
so let Thy word be sown in our midst
that the harvest may be great;
and as the banyan sends forth its
branches to take root in the soil,
so let Thy life take root in our lives.

SOUTHERN INDIAN PRAYER

Oooooooooooooooh,
The Lord is good to me,
And so I thank the Lord
For giving me the things I need,
The sun and the rain and the apple seed.
The Lord is good to me.

And every seed that grows
Will grow into a tree,
And one day soon there'll be apples there,
For everyone in the world to share.
The Lord is good to me.

When I wake up each morning,
I'm happy as can be,
Because I know that with God's care
The apple trees will still be there.
The Lord's been good to me.

OR, A VARIATION:

Oh, the Earth is good to me,
and so I thank the Earth for giving me
the things I need,
the sun and the rain and the apple seed.
The Earth is good to me.

TRADITIONAL AMERICAN,
"JOHNNY APPLESEED GRACE"

May your life be like a wildflower,
growing freely in the beauty and joy
of each day.

NATIVE AMERICAN PROVERB

23

I am the one whose praise echoes on high.
I adorn all the earth.
I am the breeze
that nurtures all things green.
I encourage blossoms to flourish with ripening fruits.
I am led by the spirit to feed the purest streams.
I am the rain
coming from the dew
that causes the grasses to laugh with the joy of life.
I am the yearning for good.

HILDEGARD OF BINGEN (1098–1179)

This snowy morning
That black crow I hate so much . . .
But he's beautiful!

MATSUO BASHŌ (1644–1694)

All things bright and beautiful,
All creatures great and small,
All things wise and wonderful,
The Lord God made them all.

Each little flower that opens,
Each little bird that sings,
He made their glowing colors,
He made their tiny wings.

All things bright . . .

The purple-headed mountain,
The river running by,
The sunset, and the morning,
That brightens up the sky;

All things bright . . .

The cold wind in the winter,
The pleasant summer sun,
The ripe fruits in the garden,
He made them, every one.

He gave us eyes to see them,
And lips that we might tell,
How great is God Almighty,
Who has made all things well.

CECIL FRANCES ALEXANDER (1818–1895)

25

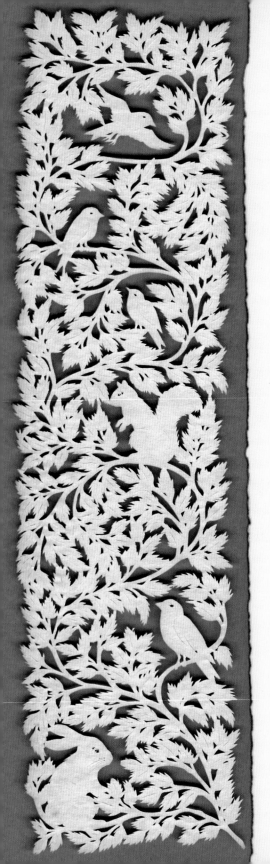

We praise you for our Brother Wind and every kind of weather, stormy or mild. For when he roars he reminds us of your might, and when he comes as a cooling breeze, he tells us of your gentleness.

Praise, too, for our ever-present Brother Air, who, though invisible, surrounds us and gives us life and breath. Truly, he is a creation in your likeness.

We praise you for Sister Water, who fills the seas and rushes down the rivers—who wells up from the earth and falls down from heaven—who gives herself that all living things may grow and be nourished.

We praise you for our Brother Fire, whose strength warms our bones and in whose resplendent dancing light we glimpse your playfulness.

We praise you for our Sister Earth, who declares your mother love for us as she sustains our bodies with food and our souls with beauty.

SAINT FRANCIS OF ASSISI (1181–1226), FROM "CANTICLE OF THE CREATURES," REIMAGINED BY KATHERINE PATERSON

To every thing there is a season, and a time to every purpose under the heaven:

A time to be born, and a time to die;
A time to plant, and a time to pluck up that which is planted;
A time to kill, and a time to heal;
A time to break down, and a time to build up;
A time to weep, and a time to laugh;
A time to mourn, and a time to dance; . . .
A time to rend, and a time to sew;
A time to keep silence, and a time to speak;
A time to love, and a time to hate;
A time of war, and a time of peace.

ECCLESIASTES 3:1–4, 7–8, KING JAMES VERSION

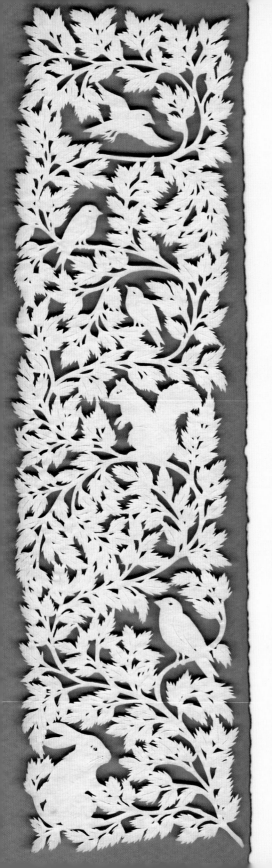

In the house made of dawn.
In the story made of dawn.
On the trail of dawn.
O, Talking God.
His feet, my feet, restore.
His limbs, my limbs, restore.
His body, my body, restore.
His voice, my voice, restore.
His mind, my mind, restore.
His plumes, my plumes, restore.
With beauty before him, with beauty before me.
With beauty behind him, with beauty behind me.
With beauty above him, with beauty above me.
With beauty below him, with beauty below me.
With beauty around him, with beauty around me.
With pollen beautiful in his voice, with pollen
    beautiful in my voice.
It is finished in beauty.
It is finished in beauty.
In the house of evening light.
From the story made of evening light.
On the trail of evening light.

NAVAJO PRAYER

To make a prairie it takes a clover and one bee,—
One clover, and a bee,
And revery.
The revery alone will do
If bees are few.

EMILY DICKINSON (1830–1886)

Not knowing when the dawn will come
I open every door;
Or has it feathers like a bird,
Or billows like a shore?

EMILY DICKINSON (1830–1886)

To see a World in a Grain of Sand
And a Heaven in a Wild Flower,
Hold Infinity in the palm of your hand
And Eternity in an hour.

WILLIAM BLAKE (1757–1827), "AUGURIES OF INNOCENCE"

29

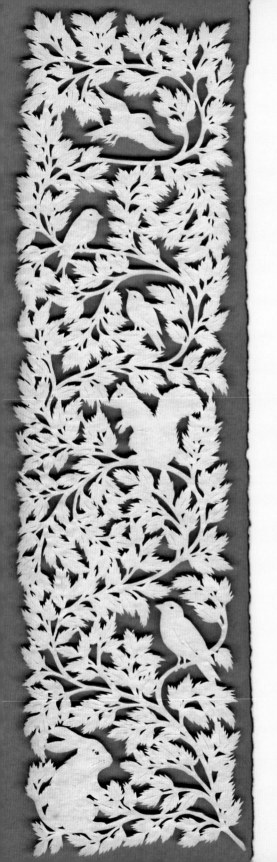

The year's at the spring
And day's at the noon;
Morning's at seven;
The hillside's dew-pearled;
The lark's on the wing;
The snail's on the thorn;
God's in his heaven—
All's right with the world!

ROBERT BROWNING
(1812–1889), *PIPPA PASSES*

How beautiful and perfect are the animals!
    How perfect is my soul!
How perfect the Earth, and the minutest thing on it!
What is called good is perfect, and what is called
    bad is just as perfect;
The vegetables and minerals are all perfect,
    and the imponderable fluids are perfect;
Slowly and surely they have passed on to this,
    and slowly and surely they yet pass on. . . .
I swear I think there is nothing but immortality!

WALT WHITMAN (1819–1892), *LEAVES OF GRASS*

I believe a leaf of grass is no less than the journey-work of the stars,
And the pismire is equally perfect, and a grain of sand, and the egg of the wren,
And the tree-toad is a chef-d'oeuvre for the highest,
And the running blackberry would adorn the parlors of heaven,
And the narrowest hinge in my hand puts to scorn all machinery,
And the cow crunching with depress'd head surpasses any statue,
And a mouse is miracle enough to stagger sextillions of infidels,
And I could come every afternoon of my life to look at the farmer's girl boiling
  her iron tea-kettle and baking shortcake.

WALT WHITMAN (1819–1892), *LEAVES OF GRASS*

Dear Father, hear and bless
Thy beasts and singing birds;
And guard with tenderness
Small things that have no words.

AUTHOR UNKNOWN

O heavenly Father, protect and bless all things
that have breath: guard them from all evil, and let
them sleep in peace.

ALBERT SCHWEITZER (WHEN A CHILD)
(1875–1965), "A CHILD'S PRAYER"

Schweitzer writes:
*"As far back as I can remember I was saddened by the amount of misery I
saw in the world around me. One thing that especially saddened me was that
the unfortunate animals had to suffer so much pain and misery. It was quite
incomprehensible to me why in my evening prayers I should pray for human
beings only. So when my mother had prayed with me and kissed me goodnight,
I used to add silently [the above] prayer that I had composed myself for
all living creatures."*

I thank You God for most this amazing
day: for the leaping greenly spirits of trees and
a blue true dream of sky; and for everything
which is natural which is infinite which is yes

E. E. CUMMINGS (1894–1962), FROM "THIS AMAZING DAY"

The Spirit Within

I must have been twelve, which was a period in my life when I seemed to have gained a bit of self-confidence and wanted to appear sophisticated. My mother had just explained to me that something I wanted was financially beyond our reach, and I sighed and said, "I guess we're poor in everything but spirit." She smiled wryly. "Spirit is the only thing the Bible tells us we *should* be poor in." She was reminding me that in the Beatitudes Jesus says, "Blessed (or happy) are the poor in spirit, for theirs is the kingdom of heaven."

But I didn't want to be poor in any-thing. I was tired of always wearing hand-me-downs and praying for years for a bicycle that when it arrived had peeling paint and faulty brakes. I cer-tainly didn't like the idea of being poor in spirit, whatever that might mean. I was rather full of myself and wanted to be noticed and admired. I didn't want to be like my nine-year-old self, so intimidated by life in America that she was the easy target of playground bullies. That shy little nobody of a person was what I imagined it meant to be poor in spirit. It didn't occur to me then, that it was my three-year-old self that was truly poor in spirit—a beloved child who had very little power or pride but whose trusting spirit was wide awake to joy and wonder.

John Greenleaf Whittier ends his poem "My Psalm" with these words:

That all the jarring notes of life
Seem blending in a psalm,
And all the angles of its strife
Slow rounding into calm.

And so the shadows fall apart,
And so the west-winds play;
And all the windows of my heart
I open to the day.

K. P.

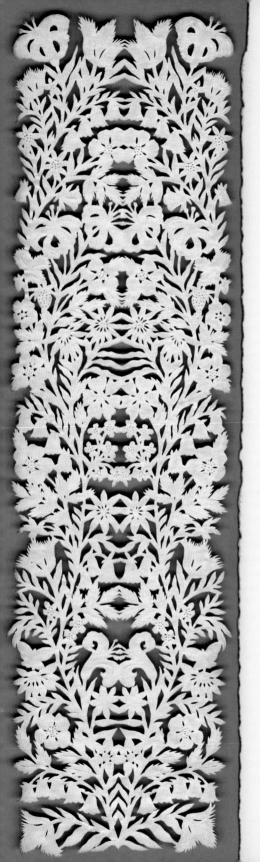

Precious Lord, take my hand
Lead me on, let me stand
I am tired, I am weak, I am worn
Through the storm,
Through the night,
Lead me on to the light.
Take my hand, precious Lord,
and lead me home.

THOMAS A. DORSEY (1899–1983)

O Lord, help me to understand that
You ain't gwine to let nuthin' come my way that
You and me can't handle together.

AUTHOR UNKNOWN

Amazing grace! How sweet the sound
That sav'd a wretch like me.
I once was lost, but now am found,
Was blind but now I see.

'Twas grace that taught my heart to fear,
And grace my fears reliev'd;
How precious did that grace appear
The hour I first believ'd!

JOHN NEWTON (1725–1807)

O God, light a candle in my heart
And sweep the darkness from Your dwelling space.
Amen.

MARIAN WRIGHT EDELMAN (B. 1939), "HOPE"

Dear Lord, be good to me. The sea is so wide
and my boat is so small.

SEAMEN'S PRAYER, ATTRIBUTED VARIOUSLY TO
IRISH OR BRETON FISHERMEN (AND MOTTO OF
THE CHILDREN'S DEFENSE FUND)

I think over again my small adventures,
My fears,
These small ones that seemed so big.
For all the vital things I had to get and to reach.
And yet there is only one great thing,
The only thing.
To live to see the great day that dawns
And the light that fills the world.

INUIT SONG

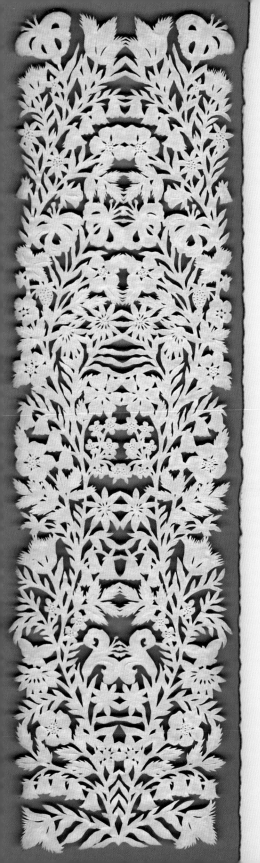

All of creation is a symphony of joy and jubilation . . .

. . . Prayer is nothing but the inhaling and exhaling of the
one breath of the universe.

HILDEGARD OF BINGEN (1098–1179), ATTRIBUTED

The best and most beautiful things in
the world cannot be seen or even touched.
They must be felt with the heart.

HELEN KELLER (1880–1968)

The Lord is my shepherd; I shall not want. He maketh
me to lie down in green pastures: he leadeth me beside
the still waters. He restoreth my soul: he leadeth me
in the paths of righteousness for his name's sake. Yea,
though I walk through the valley of the shadow of death,
I will fear no evil: for thou art with me; thy rod and thy
staff they comfort me. Thou preparest a table before me
in the presence of mine enemies: thou anointest my head
with oil; my cup runneth over. Surely goodness and mercy
shall follow me all the days of my life: and I will dwell in
the house of the Lord for ever.

PSALM 23, KING JAMES VERSION

O our Father, the Sky, hear us and make us strong.
O our Mother the Earth, hear us and give us support.
O Spirit of the East, send us your Wisdom.
O Spirit of the South, may we tread your path of life.
O Spirit of the West, may we always be ready for the long journey.
O Spirit of the North, purify us with your cleansing winds.

SIOUX PRAYER

Gratitude is from the same root word as "grace" . . .
Thanksgiving is from the same root word as "think,"
     so that to think is to thank.

WILLIS P. KING (1839–1909), "PULPIT PREACHING"

Blessed are we who can laugh at ourselves,
For we shall never cease to be amused.

AUTHOR UNKNOWN

Give me a sense of humor,
Give me the grace to see a joke,
To get some pleasure out of life
And pass it on to other folk.

AUTHOR UNKNOWN

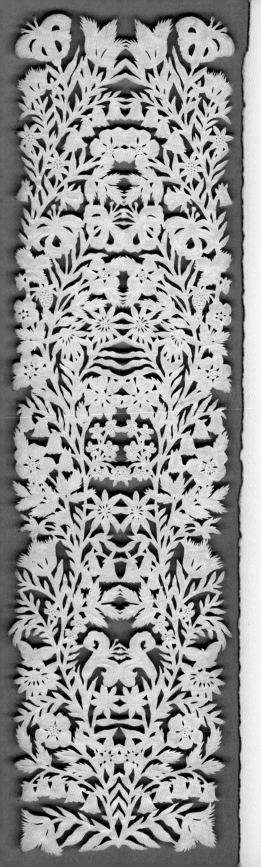

Here with flowers I interweave my friends.
Let us rejoice!
Our common house is the earth.
I am come too, here I am standing;
now I am going to forge songs,
make a stem flowering with songs,
oh my friend!
God has sent me as a messenger.
I am transformed into a poem.

NAHUATL BLESSING (CA. 1300 B.C.E.)

I salute you! There is nothing I can give you which
you have not; but there is much, very much, that, while
I cannot give, you can take.

No Heaven can come to us unless our hearts find rest
in it today. Take Heaven.

No peace lies in the future which is not hidden in the
present moment. Take Peace.

The gloom of the world is but a shadow; behind it, yet
within our reach is joy. Take joy.

. . . And so, at this Christmas time, I greet you, with
the prayer that for you, now and forever, the day
breaks and the shadows flee away.

FRA GIOVANNI GIOCONDO (CA. 1433–1515), ATTRIBUTED

When I rise up
let me rise up joyful
like a bird.

When I fall
let me fall without regret
like a leaf.

WENDELL BERRY (B. 1934), FROM "PRAYERS
AND SAYINGS OF THE MAD FARMER"

I part the out thrusting branches
and come in beneath
the blessed and the blessing trees.

Though I am silent there is singing around me.
Though I am dark there is vision around me.
Though I am heavy there is flight around me.

WENDELL BERRY (B. 1934), FROM "WOODS"

Circle of Community

I was born in China; I have lived in Japan and in six different states in America and visited more foreign countries than I can count on the fingers of both hands. And what this has taught me is how wide and rich the circle of my community is. I have met Russians and Kenyans and Iranians and Israelis and Palestinians and Cubans and Colombians and on and on—people of many cultures and colors and languages and religions—and recognized my kinship with them.

It has not always been so. When I was not quite five, war broke out between China and Japan. I was terrified of the Japanese bombers that flew over our roof to drop bombs nearby, and I was even more terrified of the soldiers who followed soon after to take over the land. I thought I hated the Japanese people.

If anyone had told me when I was nine that I would go to Japan and live there for four years, I wouldn't have believed them. But I did just that, and I came to see the Japanese people in a wholly different light. Before long I felt totally at home in Japan. At a farewell party given by one of the tiny churches in which I worked, the pastor cited a verse from the Book of Ephesians which reads, "For [Christ] is our peace, who has made us both one, and has broken down the dividing wall of hostility." And then he went on to say, "Katherine is young, I am old. She is American, I am Japanese. When she was a child of missionaries in China, I was a colonel in the army of occupation in Manchuria. She comes from the Presbyterian tradition, I come from the Pentecostal. The world would think it impossible that she and I should love each other." And yet I knew Pastor Iwaii truly cared for me.

It is an amazing experience to find yourself loved by people you thought you hated. I will always be grateful.

K. P.

Do all the good you can
By all the means you can,
In all the ways you can,
In all the places you can,
To all the people you can,
As long as ever you can.

JOHN WESLEY (1703–1791)

Khamemi savve jiva, savve jiva khamantu me
We forgive all the living beings, we seek pardon
    from all the living beings

Mitti me savva bhooesu, veram mahjjam na kenavi
We are friendly towards all the living beings,
    and we seek enmity with none

Michchhami dukkadam!
Moreover, we ask for forgiveness from all!

JAIN PRAYER OF FORGIVENESS

I have a dream today. I have a dream that one day every valley shall be exalted, every hill and mountain shall be made low; the rough places will be made plain, and the crooked places will be made straight; and the glory of the Lord shall be revealed, and all flesh shall see it together.

This is our hope. This is the faith that I go back to the South with. With this faith we will be able to hew out of the mountain of despair a stone of hope. With this faith we will be able to transform the jangling discords of our nation into a beautiful symphony of brotherhood. With this faith we will be able to work together, to pray together, to struggle together, to go to jail together, to stand up for freedom together, knowing that we will be free one day. This will be the day when all of God's children will be able to sing with new meaning:

My country, 'tis of thee, sweet land of liberty, of thee I sing:
Land where my fathers died, land of the pilgrim's pride,
From every mountainside, Let freedom ring! . . .

[W]hen we allow freedom to ring, when we let it ring from every village and every hamlet, from every state and every city, we will be able to speed up that day when all of God's children, black men and white men, Jews and Gentiles, Protestants and Catholics, will be able to join hands and sing in the words of the old Negro spiritual, "Free at last! Free at last! Thank God almighty, we are free at last!"

MARTIN LUTHER KING JR. (1924–1968)

I've got a robe, you've got a robe
All of God's children got a robe
When I get to Heaven, goin' to put on my robe
Goin' to shout all over God's Heaven.

Heav'n, Heav'n
Ev'rybody talkin' 'bout Heav'n ain't goin' there
Heav'n, Heav'n
Goin' to shout all over God's Heaven.

I've got shoes, you've got shoes
All of God's children got shoes
When I get to Heaven, goin' to put on my shoes
Goin' to walk all over God's Heaven.

I've got a song, you've got a song
All of God's children got a song
When I get to Heaven, goin' to sing a new song
Goin' to sing all over God's Heaven.

AFRICAN-AMERICAN SPIRITUAL

All God's critters got a place in the choir
Some sing low and some sing higher
Some sing out loud on the telephone wires
Some just clap their hands or paws or anything they've got now

Listen to the bass, it's the one on the bottom
Where the bullfrog croaks and the hippopotamus
Moans and groans with a big to-do
And the old cow just goes moo

The dogs and the cats, they take up the middle
Where the honeybee hums and the cricket fiddles
The donkey brays and the pony neighs
And the old gray badger sighs oh

All God's critters got a place in the choir . . .

Listen to the top where the little birds sing
On the melodies and the high notes ringing
And the hoot-owl hollers over everything
And the blackbird disagrees

Singing in the night-time, singing in the day
The little duck quacks, then he's on his way
And the otter hasn't got much to say
And the porcupine talks to himself

All God's critters got a place in the choir . . .

It's a simple song, of living sung everywhere
By the ox and the fox and the grizzly bear
The dopey alligator and the hawk above
The sly old weasel and the turtledove.

BILL STAINES (B. 1947)

47

Wa-kon'da,
here needy he stands,
and I am he.

OMAHA TRIBAL PRAYER

May all who are sick and ill
Quickly be freed from their illness,
And may every disease in the world
Never occur again.

And now so long as space endures,
As long as there are beings to be found,
May I continue likewise to remain
To soothe the sufferings of those who live.

DALAI LAMA (B. 1935)

Do your little bit of good where you are; it's those little
bits of good put together that overwhelm the world.

DESMOND TUTU (B. 1931)

I will give you a talisman . . .
Recall the face of the poorest and the weakest man
whom you may have seen and ask yourself if the step
you contemplate is going to be of any use to him.

MAHATMA GANDHI (1869–1948)

Sometimes our light goes out, but is blown again into
instant flame by an encounter with another human
being. Each of us owes the deepest thanks to those
who have rekindled this inner light.

ALBERT SCHWEITZER (1875–1965)

A circle of friends is a blessed thing.
Sweet is the breaking of bread with friends.
For the honor of their presence at our board
We are deeply grateful, Lord.

Thanks be to Thee for friendship shared,
Thanks be to Thee for food prepared.
Bless Thou the cup; bless Thou the bread;
Thy blessing rest upon each head.

WALTER RAUSCHENBACH (1861–1918)

Blessed be

ANCIENT CELTIC BLESSING

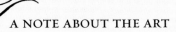

A NOTE ABOUT THE ART

The illustrations in this book were rendered in a cut-paper technique popular in early-nineteenth-century America (*Scherenschnitte*). The paper was then antiqued in a coffee solution, ironed, and illuminated with watercolor.

PERMISSIONS

Grateful acknowledgment is made to the following for permission to reprint copyrighted or controlled selections:

Page 32: "A Child's Prayer" by Albert Schweitzer. Reprinted by permission of Philosophical Library, Inc.

Page 47: "All God's Critters Got a Place in the Choir" words and music by Bill Staines. Copyright © 1978 by Mineral River Music BMI. Reprinted by permission of the author.

Page 15: "Blessing of the Stew Pot" from *Water Women*. [audiocassette] by Alla Renée Bozarth. Wisdom House, 1990. Copyright © 1990 by Alla Renée Bozarth. Reprinted by permission of the author.

Pages 16, 37: "Gratitude" and "Hope" from *I'm Your Child, God* by Marian Wright Edelman. Text © 2002 by Marian Wright Edelman. Reprinted by permission of Disney·Hyperion, an imprint of Disney Book Group, LLC and Russell & Volkening as agents for the author.

Page 40: "Here with Flowers," A Nahuatl Blessing, from *Mexico's Feasts of Life* by Patricia Quintana, with Carol Haralson. Council Oaks Books, 1989. Reprinted by permission of the publisher.

Page 24: "I am the one whose praise echoes on high" from *Meditations with Hildegard of Bingen*. Gabriele Uhlein, editor. Bear & Company/Inner Traditions, © 1983. Reprinted by permission of the publisher.

Page 45: "I Have a Dream" by Dr. Martin Luther King Jr. Copyright © 1963 Dr. Martin Luther King Jr, renewed 1991 Coretta Scott King. Reprinted by arrangement with The Heirs to the Estate of Martin Luther King Jr., c/o Writers House as agent for the proprietor, New York, NY.

Page 33: "I Thank You God" from *Xaipe: Seventy-One Poems* by E. E. Cummings. Copyright © 1926. Reprinted by permission of the publisher, W.W. Norton.

Page 22: "Morning Has Broken" by Eleanor Farjeon. Copyright © 1957. Reprinted by permission of Harold Ober Associates, Inc.

Page 12: "Mother Earth, You Who Give Us Food" from *I, Rigoberta Menchú: An Indian Woman in Guatemala*, edited and introduced by Elisabeth Burgos-Debray, translated by Ann Wright. Verso: London & New York, 1984, 2009 (first published by Editions Gallimard, 1983). Reprinted by permission of the publisher.

Page 48: "May All Who Are Sick and Ill" by The Dalai Lama, from *Prayers for Healing: 365 Blessings, Poems, and Meditations from Around the World*, edited by Maggie Oman. Conari Press, 1997. Reprinted by permission of the Office of Tibet.

Page 41: "Prayers and Sayings of the Mad Farmer" and "Woods," from *New Collected Poems* by Wendell Berry. Copyright © 2012 by Wendell Berry. Reprinted by permission of the publisher, Counterpoint.

An exhaustive effort has been made to locate all rights holders and to clear reprint permissions. If any required acknowledgments have been omitted, or any rights overlooked, it is unintentional and forgiveness is requested. If notified, the publishers will be pleased to rectify any omission in future editions.